Kni...pool

Jane Clarke and Jane Massey

In the time of the knights,

it was time for school.

Little Knight and Little Dragon were the best of friends.

They loved to have fun and adventures together,
and they couldn't wait to start school on the very same day.

On the first day of school,

But Daddy Knight took
Little Knight to Knight School
in the day time.

their daddies helped them get ready.

And Daddy Dragon took
Little Dragon to Dragon School
at night time.

School was fun!

Little Knight and Little Dragon sang funny songs,
painted fabulous pictures, and listened to fantastic stories.

And they learned what knights

and dragons should do if they ever met a princess.

Day followed night and night followed day, and Little Knight and Little Dragon hardly ever saw each other.

Little Knight and Little Dragon were sad. They both said:

I want to play with my friend!

But even at weekends it was hard to find the time.

So one day, the two friends decided to make time
for an adventure together.

After Knight School finished and before Dragon School began,
they met at the edge of the forest.

They crept into the deep **dark** **forest,** on the lookout for adventure.

A **big** eye was shining in the moonlight.

"It's a monster!"

cried Little Knight and Little Dragon.

The monster's eye came closer and closer . . .

But it wasn't a monster –
it was a little princess!

"Rescue her!" shouted Little Knight.

"Scare her!" shouted Little Dragon.

Little Princess looked at Little Knight and Little Dragon.
"I'm not scared, and I don't need rescuing!" she said.

"I'm looking for shooting stars.
Do you want to look for some too?"

Little Knight and Little Dragon gazed
up into the night sky.

It wasn't long before they spotted a shooting star.
And the more they gazed, the more they found.

They couldn't wait to tell their friends at school.

Suddenly there was a rustling in the trees . . .

"There you are!"
cried Daddy Knight
and Daddy Dragon.

"Whatever are you are doing at this time of night?"
said Daddy Knight. "We were so worried!"

"We never get to meet at school,"
Little Knight and Little Dragon explained.
"This is the only time we can get together."

Daddy Knight and Daddy Dragon looked at each other.
"It's important to make time for friends," they agreed.

So from then on, at weekends and holidays,

Little Knight and Little Dragon always had time

to have fun and adventures together.

And the two families invited teachers and school friends
(and some special royal guests) to a **party** to celebrate school
in the time of the knights.

Bouncy
Castle

Fancy Dress

Face Painting

Hook a Duck

Toffee Apples

Apple Juice

Buns

To Rob and Amy, and living happily ever after – JC
For Billy – JM

KNIGHT SCHOOL
A RED FOX BOOK 978 1 849 41501 9

Published in Great Britain by Red Fox, an imprint of Random House Children's Books
A Random House Group Company

This edition published 2012

1 3 5 7 9 10 8 6 4 2

Text copyright © Jane Clarke, 2012
Illustrations copyright © Jane Massey, 2012

Red Fox Books are published by Random House Children's Books,
61–63 Uxbridge Road, London W5 5SA

www.kidsatrandomhouse.co.uk
www.randomhouse.co.uk

Addresses for companies within The Random House Group Limited can be found at: www.randomhouse.co.uk/offices.htm

THE RANDOM HOUSE GROUP Limited Reg. No. 954009

A CIP catalogue record for this book is available from the British Library.

Printed in China

The Random House Group Limited supports The Forest Stewardship Council (FSC®), the leading
international forest certification organisation. Our books carrying the FSC label are printed on FSC® certified paper.
FSC is the only forest certification scheme endorsed by the leading environmental organisations, including Greenpeace.
Our paper procurement policy can be found at www.randomhouse.co.uk/environment

MIX
Paper from
responsible sources
FSC® C020056